Hanukkah!

by Roni Schotter ✦ illustrated by Marylin Hafner

In darkest December
Night steals in early
And whisks away the light.

But warm inside,
Mama, Papa, and Grandma Rose
Light the sun that is the menorah.

While Nora and Dan,
Ruthie and Sam
Sing a song
That is a prayer.

"Birthday!" Moe points and drops his bottle. "Hot!"
"No, Hanukkah," Sam says, "Say, 'Hanukkah,' Moe."
"Abadah, Moe," Moe says. "Abadah!" and drools on Sam's hand.

Nora and Dan, in the kitchen,
Fry some batter.
Flip, flap here.
Flip, flop there.
Potato pancakes in the air.
Latkes flying everywhere!

Ruthie, in her bedroom,
Mixes some paint.
A drop of blue,
A drop of red,
A drop of purple
On Rabbit's head.

While off in a corner, tucked away, Sam shapes a dreidel of clay.

"Top!" Moe shouts, spinning round and round.
"Yes, dreidel," Sam says. "For Hanukkah. Say 'Hanukkah,' Moe."
"Anoohah, Moe," Moe says. "Anoohah!" and drools on Sam's foot.

Then…
One by one
Their gifts in hand,
The children gather
Round.

Grandma carries her favorite dish,
Pot roast, warm, and brown, and rich.
Papa brings his salad, cool and crisp,
And Mama, her applesauce.
"Dee-licious!" Moe says.

"The latkes have landed! The latkes have landed!"
Sam shouts, holding out his plate.

Moe grabs five, unable to wait.

And, as the Hanukkah candles
Lean head to head,
So does the family…

"Ohhh!"

"Ahhh!"

"Ummm!"

"Yummm!"

"Burp!"

But wait… there's more.
There's no escape.
It's Grandma's famous lemon cake!

And cookies,
And candy,
And fruit,
And nuts,
And now *that's all*.
Enough's enough!

Time for presents
Or what's a party?
For songs…
For dances…

And something more…

Love!

Light!

Hanukkah!

"Say 'Hanukkah,' Moe," Sam says. "Come on, Moe. Say 'Hanukkah'!"

"Anoo…" Moe gurgles. "Hanu-*kkah*!"

Moe shouts and hugs Sam. "Hanukkah!"

And, as the candles burn low and lose their light,
Eight sleepy people say, "**GOOD NIGHT.**"